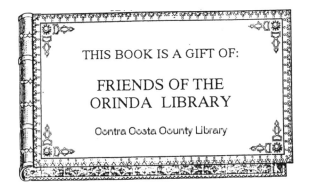

WHEN THE CHENOO HOWLS

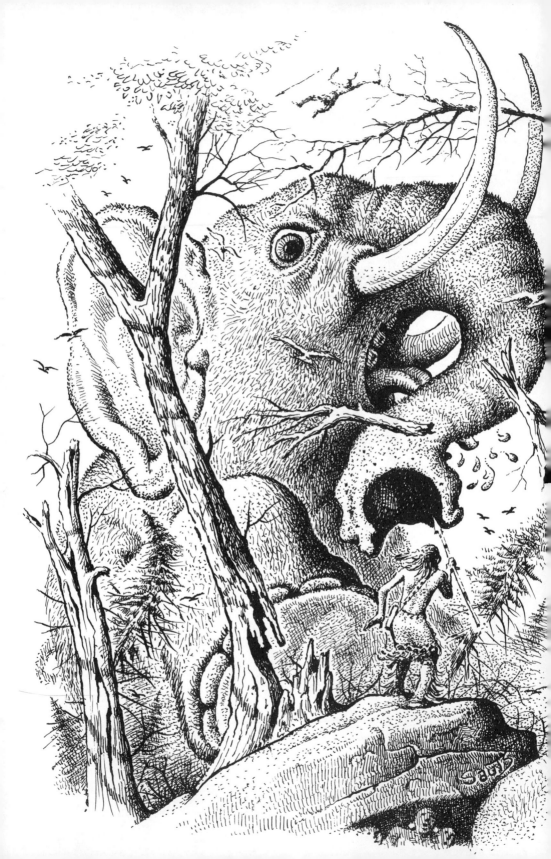

WHEN THE CHENOO HOWLS

NATIVE AMERICAN TALES OF TERROR

Joseph and James Bruchac

Illustrations by William Sauts Netamuxwe Bock

Walker and Company

New York

First published in the United States of America in 1998
by Walker Publishing Company, Inc.

Published simultaneously in Canada by Thomas Allen & Son Canada,
Limited, Markham, Ontario

Library of Congress Cataloging-in-Publication Data
Bruchac, Joseph, 1942–
When the Chenoo howls: native American tales of terror/Joseph and James
Bruchac; illustrations by William Sauts Netamux̌we Bock.
p.   cm.
Includes bibliographical references
Contents: The Stone Giant (Seneca) — The Flying Head (Seneca) — Ugly face
(Mohawk) — Chenoo (Passamaquoddy) — Amankamek (Lenape) —
Keewahkwee (Penobscot) — Yakwawiak (Lenape) — Man Bear (Oneida) —
The Spreaders (Abenaki) — Aglebemu (Penobscot) —
Big Tree People (Onondaga) — Toad Woman (Abenaki)
ISBN 0-8027-8638-3 (hardcover: alk. paper)
ISBN 0-8027-8639-1 (reinforced: alk. paper)
1. Indians of North America — Northeastern
States — Folklore.   2. Woodland Indians — Folklore.
3. Tales — Northeastern States.   4. Monsters — Juvenile literature.
[1. Woodland Indians — Folklore.   2. Indians of North
America — Northeastern States — Folklore. 3. Monsters — Folklore.
4. Folklore — Northeastern States.]   I. Bruchac, James.   II. Bock,
William Sauts, 1939–   ill.   III. Title.
E78.E2B79   1998
[398.2'089'97074] — dc21   97-48715
CIP
AC

Book design by Jennifer Ann Daddio

Printed in the United States of America

2   4   6   8   10   9   7   5   3   1

CONTENTS

AUTHORS' NOTE

In all cases, these stories are versions told in our own words of traditional tales. While we have attempted to stay true to the traditions from which these stories originate and to the many different elders who shared these stories with us over the past three decades, these are *new* tellings. Under sources, we have indicated where some of the written versions of these or similar stories can be found.

— JOSEPH AND JAMES BRUCHAC

INTRODUCTION

Legends have always played a major role in Northeast Woodland Native American culture. Through the oral tradition, legends have passed down tribal, regional, and family histories, stressed cultural philosophies, taught lessons, and amused Native audiences for thousands of years.

Having survived into the twentieth century, Native legends are now shared with Native and non-Native audiences alike. Aided by their positive ecological and social content, legends from all over Turtle Island are not only told in front of countless audiences but also appear in numerous anthologies, picture books, and novels. In this vast body of legends, however, one type of traditional tale has often been neglected, or at least misunderstood: the monster story. As long as our tales have been told, stories of monsters have played an important role.

During our childhood in the foothills of the Adirondack Mountains, my brother Jesse and I were lucky enough to have grown up hearing many Native legends. Having a storyteller as a father, on long winter nights we heard many a tale. Our favorite ones were always the monster stories. We often went to sleep on those winter nights with thoughts of Chenoos, Flying Heads, Cannibal Ogres, and Stone Giants dancing through our heads. Luckily, in most cases we took comfort in knowing these monsters were usually defeated by a brave human being—sometimes a child no older than we were then.

Indeed, in many of our traditional Native American monster legends, heroes and heroines defeat their terrible foes by using their wits and standing up against their own fears.

This is well illustrated in the stories found in this book, such as the "The Flying Head" and "The Stone Giant." The point of such stories is usually quite obvious. Clear thinking and bravery can be victorious over evil and the twisted mind.

So important was the theme of defeating monsters that it even appears in many Northeast Woodland creation stories. For example, in an Abenaki tale Gluskabe first shaped the human beings out of stone. But those giant rock creatures caused great destruction. Having hearts of stone, they had no compassion for the earth and its many living creatures. After realizing his mistake, Gluskabe destroyed them, turning them back into broken stones. Only after their defeat could he make the first Abenaki people from the ash tree. These new people, unlike the stone beings, had hearts that were green and growing, allowing them to have respect for the earth and each other.

In such legends, be they creation stories or not, the monsters are almost always defeated.

This, however, is not always the case in another type of monster story found in this book. That type is the cautionary monster story. Those unfamiliar with such tales could be in for a big shock. In these stories, the monsters often win. Their prey, more often than not, is young children. At times, these stories seem more to resemble an episode of *Tales from the Crypt* than what many have come to expect from Native American legends. Stories about creatures such as Toad Woman, who lures young children into the cedar bogs with her beautiful voice only to drown them, don't have what most would consider happy endings. Yet this type of monster tale taught the caution that, over the centuries, probably saved thousands of young lives. Despite the many romantic ideas about our northeastern wilderness, it was and continues to be riddled with danger. Indeed, in precontact times one of the leading causes of death for Native people was accidents. These accidents included drowning, falls from high places, animal attacks, and many other things that were especially dangerous for children. Tales of Toad Woman would help frighten children away from the places where potential accidents might happen — such as the marshy cedar bogs. Monsters prove to be a more effective deterrent than a parent's simple warning.

To this day on the Abenaki reserve of Odanak, stories also included in this collection are still told about the dangerous little people known as the Spreaders. These Spreaders, as the story is told to the children of the village, are said to live near a certain cliff, a cliff that in reality is a very dangerous place. Whether it be Toad Woman, Spreaders, Stone Giants, Flying Heads, or any other monsters, the images of these creatures continue, in many Native communities, to keep children away from danger.

A second use for the cautionary monster story is to warn against bad behavior. Such bad behavior may result in a monster paying a visit. "Ugly Face" and "Big Tree People" might be used by a parent or other elder when a child is acting in a disrespectful way. In the story of the Man Bear, the hero succeeds because he remembers the advice of his elders. In the tale of Keewahkwee, the rude monster fails where the polite little boy succeeds. Among Native Americans, telling a lesson story or a cautionary tale, instead of resorting to physical punishment, has always been the preferred way to discipline a child. The aim of this type of cautionary monster story is also to help an individual child recognize bad behavior before they commit it.

Within this book are a number of different monster stories that my father, Joseph Bruchac, and I have decided to share with a wider audience. Some are heroic and cautionary. Some are traditional, and even the ones that are original tell of legendary monsters well known to our various Northeast Woodland tribes. Some take place today, not just in the distant past. We want people to realize that these stories and the Native people who tell them have not vanished. Many of our traditions are as useful today as they were a hundred or a thousand years ago. So the progression of the stories in this book is from the very distant past to very recent times. Monsters and the stories that we tell about them, new and old, continue to play an important role in many Native American communities, providing amusement and instruction. It is our belief that these stories can play a similar role for non-Native readers as well.

— JAMES BRUCHAC

THE STONE GIANT

One day, long ago in an Iroquois village, the people became very troubled. In those days, there were great monsters called Stone Giants. Taller than the trees, those creatures loved to eat human beings. Spears and arrows could not hurt them, for they had skins made of flint. That day, a Stone Giant had been seen on the other side of Ne-ah-gah, the big river that flowed near the village. The people were afraid that it would soon cross that river and attack them.

Soon almost everyone in that village was talking about it. What could they do? One of the people in that village happened to be

1

Skunny-Wundy, whose name means "Cross-the-Creek." He had been given that name because he loved to play near the stream that flowed not far from their village. Skunny-Wundy knew better than anyone all of the shallow places where one could cross. Skunny-Wundy was not a big person, but he was very quick to see things.

Sitting on a rock, his stone hatchet on the ground beside him, Skunny-Wundy sat and listened quietly as he repaired a torn moccasin. That was unusual, for Skunny-Wundy loved to talk. Of all the people in that village, no one loved to joke and talk more than he did.

"Those Stone Giants are very dangerous," said one man.

"I've heard they've been known to destroy whole villages," said another.

"Who would ever be brave enough to face such a creature?" one young woman asked. "Everyone is afraid of them."

Skunny-Wundy could stand it no longer.

"I'm not afraid of that Stone Giant!" Skunny-Wundy exclaimed. He was always as quick at bragging as he was at making jokes. "I've killed dozens of Stone Giants!"

Soon people were gathered around him.

"You've killed Stone Giants?" the woman asked.

"Of course I have. I am Skunny-Wundy, the greatest of warriors!" he answered, speaking louder as the crowd around him got bigger. "I could easily take care of that Stone Giant down by the river. Stone Giants run at the very sound of my name."

Then Skunny-Wundy began to brag about his many battles with Stone Giants. Even though none of those battles had ever taken place, he described them in great detail. Before long, everyone in the village had heard his tales. As he talked, Skunny-Wundy continued to work on his moccasin. When the final stitch had been sewn, Skunny-Wundy looked up. To his surprise, all of the people in the village had disappeared.

"Where did everyone go?"

Skunny-Wundy walked toward the main longhouse. As he approached, he heard the sound of many voices coming from inside. Apparently, they were having some sort of meeting.

"I wonder what they're talking about?" Skunny-Wundy said.

Just as he said that, the people began to come out of the lodge. All of them nodded and smiled at him. The last to come out was one of the village elders, who walked right over to Skunny-Wundy.

"After hearing of your many battles, the whole village has decided you should be the one to confront the Stone Giant," the old man said.

Skunny-Wundy had put himself on the spot. Everyone in the village was looking at him, waiting for his reply.

"I . . . would be honored," he said.

Skunny-Wundy picked up his hatchet, stuck it into his belt, and started through the woods toward the river. As he walked, he scolded himself for having such loose lips. Skunny-Wundy was so upset that he didn't realize how fast he was walking. Before he knew it, he had reached the edge of the river. Looking over at him from the opposite shore stood the Stone Giant.

"Stay where you are! I'm coming over to eat you!" the Stone Giant roared.

Skunny-Wundy froze.

The Stone Giant slowly waded into the water, heading straight toward him. However, when it reached the deepest part of the river, the Stone Giant's head went completely underwater. Skunny-Wundy got an idea. Running upstream to the shallow part of the river, he quickly crossed over. Before the Stone Giant reached the shore, Skunny-Wundy was standing on the opposite side, directly across from him.

The Stone Giant looked around in confusion.

"Hey," Skunny-Wundy yelled, "I thought you were coming to get me!"

The Stone Giant turned back toward the river, a confused and angry look on its face. Wading in as before, it headed once again toward Skunny-Wundy. And, just as before,

Skunny-Wundy ran to the shallow place and crossed the river. When the Stone Giant came out again, Skunny-Wundy stood on the other side.

"What's the matter, are you scared of me? Why haven't you come over here?" he yelled.

"I'm going to rip you to pieces, little man!!!"

The Stone Giant howled as it entered the water for the third time, totally unaware of the way Skunny-Wundy was tricking it.

"Sooner or later," Skunny-Wundy said to himself as he crossed the river yet again, "this not-so-smart Stone Giant will get tired of this and go away."

On his fifth trip, however, Skunny-Wundy's hatchet fell from his belt and was left behind. When the Stone Giant came out of the water, that hatchet was the first thing it saw.

"What is this?" the stone giant growled. It

bent over to pick up the hatchet. Watching from the opposite shore, Skunny-Wundy feared his trick was over. He hid behind a big tree.

"Hah! This could not hurt anything!" the Stone Giant rumbled, licking the hatchet's blade. "It is not even sharp!"

The Stone Giant threw Skunny-Wundy's little hatchet at a nearby tree. To the surprise of the Stone Giant — and Skunny-Wundy — when the hatchet struck the tree, it split that tree right in half.

"What is this?" the Stone Giant said, totally baffled. It reached down and picked up the hatchet again. This time it threw the hatchet at a huge boulder on the opposite side of the stream. As soon as that hatchet struck the boulder, the huge stone, too, was split in half. It was then that Skunny-Wundy remembered two things about Stone Giants. The first was that the saliva of a Stone Giant was very powerful. If a Stone Giant licked something, whatever it licked would have great power, too. The second thing Skunny-Wundy remembered was that Stone Giants are very stupid. This one was obviously so stupid that it did not even realize it was the one who had made that hatchet so powerful.

"That hatchet has great power," the Stone Giant growled. "Whoever owns it must be a great warrior."

Skunny-Wundy stepped out from behind the big tree. He walked over to the split rock, reached down, and picked up his hatchet.

"Ah," Skunny-Wundy said, "here is my hatchet. I must have dropped it."

"Who *are* you?" the Stone Giant asked. There was a frightened look on its face.

"I am the great warrior Skunny-Wundy. If you do not leave here for good I will split you in half!" Skunny-Wundy lifted his hatchet up over his head.

"Great warrior, do not kill me. I will go away," the Stone Giant rumbled. "I will never come back."

Then the Stone Giant turned and ran as fast it could away from the river.

Skunny-Wundy watched with a big smile

on his face. When he got back to the village, he would have yet another story to tell about defeating a Stone Giant. But this story would be true, and his magic hatchet would prove it.

THE STONE GIANT (SENECA)

Skunny-Wundy is one of the favorite trickster heroes of traditional Seneca tales. He is often described as boastful and vain. There are aspects of Skunny-Wundy's character that get him into trouble—aspects that it would not be wise to copy. However, Skunny-Wundy, whose name means "Cross-the-Creek," is also clever and resourceful. In more than one story he defeats a Stone Giant, a monster whose skin is as hard as flint. The Seneca name for Stone Giant, in fact, is Genonsgwa, or "Flint Coat." But a flexible hero like Skunny-Wundy is always a match for someone as stiff as a Stone Giant.

Sources:

Iroquois Folk Lore, by William M. Beauchamp (Port Washington, N.Y.: Kennikat Press, 1965; reissue of 1922 edition).

Legends of the Longhouse, by Jesse J. Cornplanter (Port Washington, N.Y.: Kennikat Press, 1938).

Seneca Myths and Folk Tales, by Arthur C. Parker (Buffalo, N.Y.: Buffalo Historical Society, 1923).

THE FLYING HEAD

One day, long ago, a Mohawk woman was out gathering berries in the forest. She had traveled far from her lodge, with her baby strapped to her back. Her basket almost full, the woman had just turned to head home when she heard the sound of snapping branches and rustling leaves overhead.

As the sound got closer and closer, the woman soon realized it was the sound of a Flying Head. She looked up, and a chill went down her spine as she dropped the berries she had been picking. She could see the monster flying through the sky. She could see the gleam of its big sharp teeth. A giant head with long, flowing hair and no body, it had two huge paws, like those of a giant bear, that stuck out from each side of its neck. The woman took a deep breath. She knew that she and her baby were in great danger. Flying Heads had huge appetites. They were so greedy that they would eat just about anything in the forest, especially human beings.

Although it had not yet seen her through the thick branches of the trees, she knew that it was already following her scent. Soon it would fly down below the branches and follow her trail. She knew she would not be able to outrun it, and she feared for her life and the life of her baby. But she still was able to think fast. If the Flying Head was coming down for her, she would escape by going up. With her baby on her back, the woman quickly ran to a big pine tree. She leaped up to grab a branch above her head, pulled herself and her baby up into the tree, and began to climb.

No sooner had she reached a high branch than the Flying Head came into view below. Flying along close to the ground, it sniffed madly through the leaves of the forest floor. Doing her best to be quiet, the woman watched from above as the Flying Head got closer and closer. Soon it was directly below her. Its face to the ground, the Flying Head quickly worked its way around the base of the tree. Her scent ended at the bottom of the tree, and the Flying Head was now confused. It never thought of looking up. It seemed as if it might give up and go in pursuit of easier prey.

But just as the Flying Head was about to move on, the woman's small child reached out for a pine cone on a nearby branch, pulling it loose. The cone, though, was too big for the child's tiny hand. It fell down, hitting several tree limbs on the way down, and struck the monster right on top of its head. The Flying Head immediately looked up. When it spotted the woman and her child, the monster let out an ear-piercing scream.

"RAAAAAAAAAHHHHHHHHHHH!!"

Like an arrow from a bow, the Flying Head shot up toward the woman. The woman thought they were about to be devoured. But in its fury, the head flew so fast that *Bam!* it smashed into a giant tree limb, knocking itself unconscious.

As the monster fell to the ground below with a great thump, the woman quickly climbed down the tree and ran toward her lodge as fast as she could, her baby still strapped to her back But the woman knew it wouldn't be long before the Flying Head was back on her trail.

Sure enough, all too soon, she heard its cry once again.

"RAAAAAAAAAAHHHHHHHHHHHH!!"

Hearing its screams and the sound of breaking branches and rustling leaves grow closer and closer, the woman looked around. There was only one thing she could try now. She turned off the trail and entered a patch of thick brush and briars.

"RAAAAAAAAAAHHHHHHHHHHHH!!"

The Flying Head screamed as it saw the woman picking her way through the brambles. Picking up speed, it crashed into the thick brush — only to find its hair completely tangled in the maze of branches and prickly briars. As it struggled to free itself, the Flying Head's hair became more and more tangled. Seeing this, the woman turned and ran as fast as she could toward her lodge. Totally exhausted, she finally reached the place in the forest where their longhouse stood in a small clearing.

"*Wu?*" she called.

But no one answered. She looked inside. Her husband had not yet returned from hunting. She looked back toward the forest. Seeing nothing following her, she breathed a sigh of relief. It seemed that the Flying Head was no longer after her.

Entering her lodge, the woman put her baby down beside the fire. Then she sat for a time with her eyes closed, catching her breath. They were alive. They had escaped the monster.

As her breath slowed and she became calm, she realized how hungry she was. Having dropped the berries in the forest, she looked around the lodge for something that she and her baby could eat. Since her husband had not yet returned from hunting, all that she could find was a handful of chestnuts. Sitting

down in the center of her lodge, she took a stick and stirred the still-burning coals of her fire. Dropping the handful of chestnuts among the coals, she watched them carefully.

Meanwhile, back in the forest, the Flying Head had freed itself and was back on the woman's trail. It followed her scent through the forest until it reached the small clearing where her lodge stood. Then the hungry monster flew up onto the roof and looked down into the lodge through the smoke hole.

Unaware of the danger above her, the woman gently reached in among the coals. She pulled out one of the now roasted chestnuts, which looked like a blackened glowing coal. Breaking it open, she put it into her mouth.

Looking down from the smoke hole above, the Flying Head was astonished.

"What is this?" it thought. "Fire is good to eat? I must try some!"

Swooping down through the smoke hole, the Flying Head knocked the woman aside. It scooped up all of the glowing coals in its huge paws and greedily gulped them down.

"AAAAAAAHHHHHHWEEEEEEEEEE!!!!!!!" It screamed as the hot coals burned the inside of its mouth.

With gusts of smoke flowing from its mouth, the Flying Head shot up and out of the smoke hole. Away it flew, never to be seen again. So it was that the Flying Head was defeated by its own greed.

THE FLYING HEAD (SENECA)

The Flying Head is a monster sometimes equated with the whirlwind or the tornado. Telling of such creatures, "somewhere out there in the forest," was one way to keep children relatively close to home. Like all monsters, this one has a weakness—its insatiable appetite. The Flying Head, or Dagwaynonyent, as it is called in Seneca, is also often described as not being very bright. The brave woman of this story escapes because of her own determination and the monster's greed.

Sources:

Iroquois Folk Lore, by William M. Beauchamp (Port Washington, N.Y.: Kennikat Press, 1965; reissue of 1922 edition).

Legends of the Longhouse, by Jesse J. Cornplanter (Port Washington, N.Y.: Kennikat Press, 1938).

Seneca Myths and Folk Tales, by Arthur C. Parker (Buffalo, N.Y.: Buffalo Historical Society, 1923).

UGLY FACE

On a cold and windy night during the winter moon, almost everyone in the Mohawk village of Kahnesatake was asleep. Everyone, that is, except for Blue Sky and his mother, Looking Far. Since his father had left for a hunting trip three days before, Blue Sky had disobeyed his mother more and more. On the first day, shortly after his father had left, Blue Sky had refused to help his mother with the firewood. On the second day, Blue Sky and several of his friends had journeyed far from the village without Looking Far's permission, returning well past dark. Now it was very late on the third night, and Blue Sky refused to go to sleep.

"My son, for the last time, will you please come to bed?" Looking Far said, trying not to wake the others in the longhouse.

"I'm old enough to stay up as late as I want," Blue Sky responded from the place where he sat by the fire pit in the middle of the longhouse.

"Why have you continued to disobey me?" Looking Far asked in an angry voice.

His back toward his mother, Blue Sky did not even answer her.

"My son, if you continue to act this way I will have to tell Ugly Face," Blue Sky's mother said, now very angry. Outside, the wind began to blow even harder.

Dropping his stick into the fire, Blue Sky slowly turned the side of his face toward his mother.

"Who is this Ugly Face?" he asked in a sarcastic tone.

"Ugly Face is a monster so terrible that anyone who sees his face never lives to tell anyone about it."

As Looking Far spoke, a sudden gust of

wind slipped threw the cracks in the elm bark shingles. Chilling Blue Sky's bare back, the wind caused the fire to dance madly.

"I don't believe it," Blue Sky responded as he reached for his bearskin robe. "Who told you about this monster?"

"My mother told me once when I was really bad. Ugly Face comes closer whenever children disobey their parents."

"That story doesn't scare me." Blue Sky turned away and placed another piece of wood on the fire.

"I'm warning you. If you don't listen to me and come to bed, I swear I will tell Ugly Face," Looking Far persisted.

"You are the one with the ugly face," Blue Sky said. Then he laughed.

Looking Far got up from the bedrack, wrapped a long fur around her body, and walked to the eastern door of the longhouse.

"Ugly Face! There is a very bad child in this longhouse. His name is Blue Sky!" she shouted out into the night.

Blue Sky paid no attention. Instead, he

picked up another long stick and began poking at the fire once again. As his mother walked by, Blue Sky hit her on the back of her leg with the stick.

"Stop bothering me. Go back to bed," he said in a defiant voice.

Looking Far's face became dark with anger. She walked once again toward the longhouse door. She took a deep breath, thrust the doorskin aside, and leaned out.

"Ugly Face! This is Looking Far. I am Blue Sky's mother! He is getting ready for you to come and take him away from here forever!" she yelled.

A freezing wind suddenly blew snow through the open door.

"Be quiet, Mother," Blue Sky said, without even looking around. "There is no such being as Ugly Face. You are not frightening me."

Walking up behind him, Looking Far quickly grabbed hold of Blue Sky's arm and lifted him to his feet. By now, several people in the longhouse had been awakened by all the commotion.

"Let go of me!" Blue Sky yelled.

Looking Far paid no attention. Still holding onto his arm, she walked toward the eastern door of the longhouse for the third time. Dragging his feet, kicking and striking at his mother with his free hand, Blue Sky struggled the whole way. Lifting up the thick skin covering the door, his mother pushed him out of the lodge. Off balance, Blue Sky stumbled forward, falling into a huge snowbank.

"Ugly Face! Come and get him!" she called, the cold air stinging her face. Turning around, she walked back into the lodge, the heavy doorskin falling closed behind her.

"What is wrong, my sister?" one of Blue Sky's uncles asked as she walked back toward her bedrack.

"It is Blue Sky. He just won't listen to me," Looking Far responded with tears in her eyes.

"If being thrown out into the snow didn't work, I could talk with him when he comes back in," said his uncle.

"That would be good. Thank you."

Blue Sky's mother looked toward the door. Surely he would come back into the lodge soon. She went over and placed some more wood on the fire while keeping her eyes on the door. There was still no sign of her disobedient son.

Looking Far walked back over to the door of the longhouse and looked out into the darkness. The wind was no longer blowing. All was very quiet. The moonlight that shone down onto the snow showed where Blue Sky's footprints led to the snowbank and ended. No tracks led back to the door. There were no other tracks to be seen.

"Blue Sky, where are you?" she cried into the night. But there was no response.

Blue Sky was never seen again.

UGLY FACE (MOHAWK)

Ugly Face, who is called Akon:wara' in Mohawk, is a monster so terrible that no one who sees him ever lives to describe him. Disobedient Mohawk children are still sometimes threatened with Ugly Face. A contemporary telling of this story exists in Mohawk in which the little boy has been spoiled by watching too much television and no longer believes in traditional stories. He defies his grandmother when she threatens him with this monster. The results are just the same as in our telling, set in a longhouse of long ago.

Sources:

Unpublished oral tradition: told by Chief Phil Tarbell of the Akwesasne Mohawk Nation.

Published version in bilingual Mohawk/English by Mae Montour in *Kanien'Keha' Okara'shon:'A* (Mohawk Stories), Bull. 427, New York State Museum, Albany, N.Y., 1976.

THE CHENOO

Long ago, during the Moon of Falling Leaves, a woman and her two brothers traveled to the north to set up a hunting camp. Hoping to bring back enough furs and meat for the winter, they went far away from their village, much farther than anyone had gone in a long time.

During the first two days after making camp the hunting was very good. Each day the two brothers would go hunting. The sister, whose name was Nolka, would stay behind to tend their camp and prepare any game caught the day before. On the third day, however, while out hunting, the brothers came across a very large set of footprints. Those footprints were over two feet long and ten feet apart. Kneeling down, Awasos, the older of the two brothers, carefully inspected each track.

"Great-grandfather told me of a creature that makes tracks like this. It is called a Chenoo." Awasos lifted his head to scan the forest around them.

"Yes, I remember," answered Kasko, Awasos's younger brother. "He said they were giant cannibals with sharp teeth and hearts made of ice. Consuming the spirit of a human being makes them stronger."

Looking closer at the tracks, the two men realized the huge footprints were headed in the direction of their camp.

"We must return and check on our sister," said Awasos. Both men began to run back toward camp.

Meanwhile, back at camp, unaware of any danger, Nolka was busy cleaning an elk hide. Several yards away, in a large fire pit, a pile of rocks was being heated up for her brothers' evening sweat lodge.

Having finished the hide, Nolka slowly stood up to add more wood to the fire. As she did so, she heard a sudden sound of breaking branches. She turned and looked up. There stood a huge Chenoo. Its large gray body was covered with pine pitch and leaves, and it wore a necklace of human skulls. Its legs and arms were as thick as tree stumps. Its open mouth revealed a sharp set of teeth, and its eyes were darker than a starless night. The Chenoo raised its arms, preparing to grasp Nolka in its long, bony fingers.

Knowing there was nowhere to hide, Nolka thought quickly.

"Grandfather!" she said with a smile. "Where have you been?"

"GRANDFATHER?" the Chenoo growled. It stopped in its tracks and looked confused. No human being had ever dared to speak to it this way before.

"Yes, Grandfather. I have been waiting here all day for you. Don't you even remember me?" Nolka said. There was a long pause. Nolka did her best to appear calm.

"Granddaughter?!" roared the Chenoo. "I have a granddaughter?!"

"Yes, of course you do. I have been preparing this sweat lodge for you all day," Nolka said, motioning toward the large pile of rocks glowing in the fire. She hoped to delay the Chenoo from trying to eat her until her brothers returned from hunting. So far the plan was working.

"Grandfather, please come into the lodge," she said, lifting up the door flap.

"Thank you, Granddaughter," the Chenoo rumbled as it walked over to the sweat lodge and bent down. Crawling in on its hands and knees, the giant squeezed through the door. Sitting down, his legs around the fire pit, the Chenoo filled the entire lodge.

Walking over to the fire, Nolka picked up a large forked stick and carried one hot rock after another and began placing them in the center of the lodge. She was just pulling another rock out of the fire when she heard someone coming.

"Sister, what are you doing?" called

Awasos as he and Kasko, both completely out of breath, came running into the clearing.

"We saw huge tracks headed toward our camp," Kasko said. "We were afraid that you—"

Nolka held up a hand to her mouth, and her brothers stopped talking. She looked over toward the lodge.

"Our grandfather has finally arrived!" Nolka said. "Come and greet him." Then she picked up another glowing rock. As she walked over to the lodge, her brothers, totally confused, followed her.

"Grandfather, your grandsons have returned to greet you," said Nolka to the Chenoo, through the door of the lodge.

"GRANDSONS? I HAVE GRANDSONS?" roared the Chenoo. Looking into the lodge, Awasos and Kasko could not believe it. There sat the very same monster whose tracks they had seen headed toward camp.

"HELLO, MY GRANDSONS!" the Chenoo rumbled.

"Oh, ah, yes. Hello, grandfather . . . it is

good to see you," Kasko said, after being nudged in the ribs by Nolka.

"THIS LODGE FEELS GOOD. BRING ME MORE ROCKS!"

"Yes, Grandfather," Kasko said.

The two men and their sister piled one glowing rock after another in the center of the lodge. Then, after placing a large birch-bark bucket full of water just inside the door of the lodge, they closed the flap. Moments later, a loud hissing sound came from inside the lodge as the Chenoo began to pour water on the rocks.

"Now is our chance to make a run for it," Nolka whispered to her brothers. The three of them began to quietly sneak out of camp. But they had not moved quickly enough.

"MORE ROCKS! BRING ME MORE ROCKS! OPEN THE DOOR!" roared the Chenoo.

Nolka ran over and swung open the flap of the lodge. Awasos and Kasko proceeded to bring in four more loads of rocks. Then, after the fourth load, the flap to the lodge was again closed. As soon as the door was closed, the sound of hissing steam came again from within the lodge. And just as before, just when they began to sneak away, the Chenoo shouted for them again.

"OPEN THE DOOR. MORE ROCKS, MORE WATER!"

"Yes, Grandfather. We are coming!"

Quickly Awasos and Kasko brought more rocks as Nolka ran to a nearby stream to refill the birch-bark bucket. When they opened the door to the lodge, huge gusts of steam flowed out so thickly that the only thing in the lodge they could see was the Chenoo's huge arm as it reached out to grab the freshly filled bucket of water.

Closing the flap again, all three siblings agreed it was no use trying to run. The Chenoo would only call for them again. And sure enough, it did.

"OPEN THE DOOR. MORE ROCKS. MORE WATER."

This time, they brought in every rock from the fire, even the rocks from the fire circle. They hoped the heat would be so great that the Chenoo would pass out. Standing by the lodge, they listened closely. But, to their surprise, as the hissing sound of the water hitting the rocks got louder and louder, the Chenoo began to sing.

"WAY-YAA, WAY-YAA, WAY-YAA, HOOO!!

WAY-YAA, WAY-YAA, WAY-YAA, HOOO!!"

Then it paused to pour more water on the rocks before it sang again.

"WAY-YAA, WAY-YAA, WAY-YAA, HOOO!!

WAY-YAA, WAY-YAA, WAY-YAA, HOOO!!"

This time, as the Chenoo sang, they noticed that its voice did not seem as loud. Again they heard the sounds of steam rising as water was poured on the stones.

"WAY-YAA, WAY-YAA, WAY-YAA, HOOO!!

WAY-YAA, WAY-YAA, WAY-YAA, HOOO!!"

That voice was much softer now, so soft that it sounded like the voice of an old man.

"WAY-YAA, WAY-YAA, WAY-YAA, HOOO!!

Way-yaa, way-yaa, way-yaa, hooo!!"

Then it was silent.

"Grandchildren, open the door," a little voice called from inside the sweat lodge.

Awasos lifted up the door flap. A huge gust of steam blew out from the lodge, knocking him backward. As the steam rose into the air, a little old man crawled out from the lodge. As he stood up, the little old man began to cough. He coughed and coughed until he coughed up a huge piece of ice in the shape of a human heart. Falling to the ground, the heart-shaped piece of ice that was the bad spirit of the Chenoo shattered on a rock.

"Thank you, my grandchildren. You have saved me. I am no longer a monster. Now I am truly your grandfather," said the old man with a smile.

So Nolka and her two brothers took the old man who had been a Chenoo as their grandfather. They brought him back to their village, where he quietly and peacefully lived out the rest of his days.

CHENOO (PASSAMAQUODDY)

The cannibal giant whose heart is made of ice is called by many different names among the northern people where winter is the most dangerous time of year. This creature, who is sometimes described as a human being transformed into a monster, howls like the storm wind and pursues its prey. But if its heart can be melted, it may be turned back into a person. A very similar being is called Windigo by the Cree.

Sources:

"Passamaquoddy Texts," by John D. Prince, American Ethnological Society, *Publications* 10 (1921).

The Algonquin Legends of New England, by Charles G. Leland (Boston: Houghton and Mifflin, 1884).

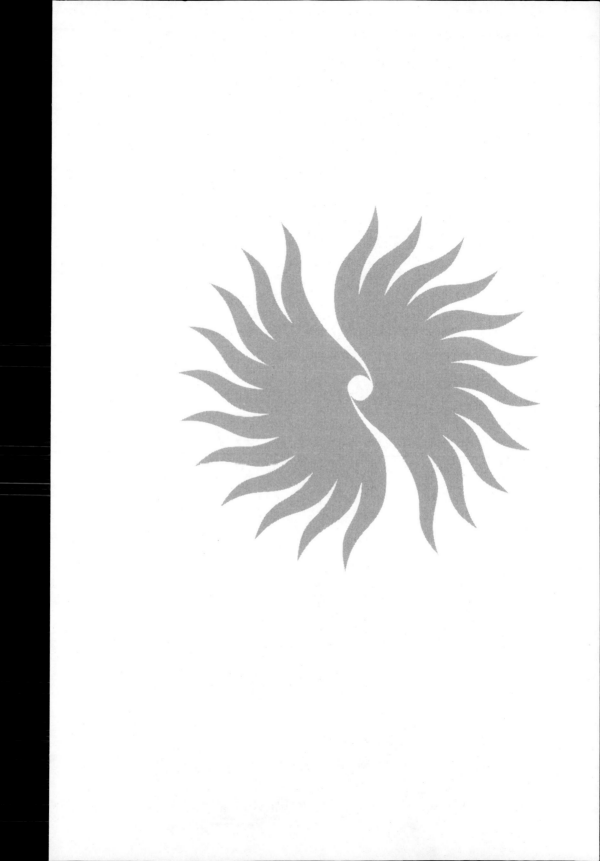

AMANKAMEK

A young woman was walking through the woods. She was on her way back to her village.

"Come here," a voice said from close behind her.

That voice frightened her. Perhaps it was the voice of Mamuui, the Eater, the one who hunts for human beings. She was about to run when she heard that voice again.

"I will not hurt you. Listen."

Then she heard the sound of a flute. She turned around to look. A young man she had never seen before sat on a fallen birch tree. He was dressed in new buckskin clothing, and that clothing was all decorated with so much quill work that it glittered in the light. The song he was playing on his flute was pleasing to her ears. He was a fine-looking young man who was pleasing to her eyes.

When he finished his song, he looked right at her and asked, "Where are you going?"

"I have just spent some time in the forest. I am going back to my village now," she answered.

"Would you like to come with me?" he said, holding out his hand.

"Yes," she said. She forgot that she was on her way home. It seemed as if he was the only thing that she could see and that his voice was the only thing she could hear. "I will come with you."

"That is good. I want you to meet my grandmother."

He took her hand, and they walked toward the river. But as they walked, the young woman noticed that things looked different. They were going down a steep hill that she had never seen before, and there was mist all around them. There were no trees, and the earth under their feet was all sand. At last they came to a cave where an old woman sat.

"Granddaughter," the old woman said, "come and sit here beside me."

"Are you hungry?" said the young man. "I will hunt for food. What kind of meat do you like?"

"I like deer meat," said the young woman.

"Then I will bring you some." The young man picked up a spear and walked off until he disappeared in the mist. Soon he came  back, carrying a deer over his shoulders.

The young woman was pleased. Not only was this young man handsome, he was also a good hunter.

"I am Red Flower. What is your name?" she asked.

"I am Amankamek," he said.

Red Flower thought that the name

sounded familiar, but she could not remember why. There were many things she could not remember. She could not remember where she had been going when she met Amankamek. She could not remember her own village.

Each day, Amankamek asked her what she wanted to eat. Each day he brought back whatever she asked him to hunt.

"While I am gone," he told Red Flower, "you may walk around. But do not go too far. And if you see even a small cloud in the sky, come back here quickly and hide in the cave."

Red Flower did as she was told. She remained in the cave with Amankamek's grandmother. She was respectful to the old woman and helped her in any way that she could. But even though the old woman was kind to her in return, Red Flower was not completely happy.

Amankamek provided her with plenty to eat. But it was cold inside the cave, and it seemed as if she could always hear strange voices at night, whispering all around her in the darkness. Red Flower began to remember her family, and she grew sad. The old woman saw this.

"Granddaughter," said the old woman one day when Amankamek was out hunting, "are you not feeling well?"

"Grandmother," Red Flower said, "I am feeling lonesome. I miss my mother."

The old woman looked at her for a long time. "Granddaughter," she said at last, "it is not right that Amankamek keeps you here. He is my grandson, but still I will help you. To-morrow, when he asks you what you want to eat, name an animal that will be difficult for him to find."

The next morning, as always, Amankamek asked Red Flower, "What would you like to eat?"

"I would like to eat the meat of a black elk that has one horn and a white spot on its shoulder."

"Ah," Amankamek said. "It will not be easy, but I will bring you what you want." Then, as always, he walked off and disappeared into the mist.

"Look at me, Granddaughter," the old woman said. Her voice sounded strange.

Red Flower turned to look. The old woman's face was growing smooth and round, and her arms and legs were shrinking as her body grew longer. When it was done, she had turned into a great horned snake.

"This is how we truly are," the old woman snake said. "Now I will help you escape from Amankamek. Climb onto my back."

Red Flower climbed onto the back of the old woman snake. It began to carry her up until they reached the surface of the river. Red Flower realized then where they had been. The cave was on the bottom of the river. The old woman snake began to swim for the shore, which was very far away.

"Granddaughter, do you see any clouds in the sky?" said the old woman snake.

"I see one small cloud far behind us," said Red Flower.

"Then I must swim faster," said the old woman snake.

"Now I see more clouds, and they are getting larger."

"I must swim very fast now," the old woman snake said.

Red Flower looked back. There were twelve clouds in the sky, and they were coming swiftly toward them. Suddenly something lifted up from the waves close behind them. It was the head of another horned snake, even larger than the old woman snake. It held in its jaws a black elk with one horn and a spot on its shoulder.

"Amankamek is close behind us," Red Flower said. "Swim faster."

"Granddaughter, where are the clouds now?" said the old woman snake.

"They are right overhead," said Red Flower.

"Then I must dive underwater," said the old woman snake. She dove out from under Red Flower just as lightning began to strike the water all around them.

Red Flower found herself underwater. She

could see the old woman snake swimming away, deeper and deeper, safe from the lightning.

Red Flower thought she would drown when a strong hand grabbed her wrist and pulled her up onto the bank of the river. A tall man dressed in red buckskin stood there. Eleven other men who looked just like him stood close behind him.

"Little one," the tall man said in a booming voice, "you have helped us. You brought the monster up so that we could strike it with our spears. You see?" he said, pointing with his lips toward the body of the great horned snake that they had pulled up out of the water. It was Amankamek.

Red Flower knew who the twelve men were. They were the Thunder Brothers, the ones who fly on the clouds seeking out the monsters that bother the people and striking them with their spears of lightning. Of all beings, they are the only ones who hunt for the great horned snakes.

"Grandfathers," she said, "I thank you."

So it was that Red Flower was saved from Amankamek, the giant horned snake, and returned to her own people. From that day on she was always a friend of Thunder.

AMANKAMEK (LENAPE)

In some stories this creature is dangerous to the people. In others, it befriends and helps human beings. The underwater snake is usually described as a serpent as large as a whale, with either one or two horns on top of its head. The horns of the snake are reputed to have great power and can be used to heal the sick. The horned snake is the mortal enemy of the Thunder Brothers, and when lightning strikes over the deep water, it is said that Thunder is fighting with the underwater snake.

Sources:

The Algonquin Legends of New England, by Charles G. Leland (Boston: Houghton and Mifflin, 1884).

Folk Medicine of the Delaware, by Gladys Tantaquidgeon, Pennsylvania Historical and Museum Commission Anthropological Series (1972).

The White Deer and Other Stories Told by the Lenape, by John Bierhorst (New York: William Morrow and Company, Inc., 1995).

The Grandfathers Speak: Native American Folk Tales of the Lenape People, by Hitakonanu'laxk (Interlink Books, 1994).

KEEWAHKWEE

Long ago, a boy lived alone in a cave in the forest with someone who said that she was his older sister. However, she always sat with her back to him, and she kept her long, tangled black hair brushed over her face so that he could not even see her eyes.

Older Sister never left the cave. Each day she would send the boy, whose name was Little Weasel, out to get food. Aside from making him new moccasins whenever the old ones wore out, she provided nothing for him. Little Weasel was a very good trapper. All through the day he would check his snares for animals and birds and bring whatever he caught back to the cave. Then he would divide the game into two piles. The small pile would be for him.

"You eat now," Older Sister would say in her strange voice. "I will eat after you are sleeping."

Then Little Weasel would cook his food, eat it, and go to bed next to the fire with his blanket pulled over his head. He always kept his blanket tight over his head, as Older Sister told him.

"If you do not cover your head," she said, "the sparks from the fire will burn your face."

Each morning she would do a very strange thing. With her back toward him, she would reach out one hand.

"Let me see how fat your arm is now, little brother." Then she would squeeze his arm. "Ah," she would say, "not yet fat enough."

It bothered Little Weasel that Older Sister did this. So he decided he would no longer allow her to really feel his arm. Instead, because she did not turn around to look, he would hold out a stick for her to squeeze.

"Ah," she began to say, "so thin and bony. Not yet fat enough."

One day, as Little Weasel checked his traps, he found a rabbit caught by one leg.

"If you let me go," the rabbit said, "I will tell you something that you need to know."

"I will do as you ask," Little Weasel said. Then he removed the snare from the rabbit's leg.

"The one who calls herself your older sister is not really your relative," the rabbit said. "She stole you from your grand-father when you were a baby. I know you are his grandson, for you have one dark eye and one light eye, 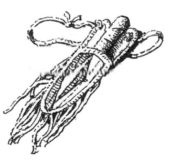 just as he does. Watch her when she eats to-night, and you will see."

That night, after he ate, Little Weasel curled up next to the fire and covered his head with his deerskin blanket. But he took his knife and put a hole in his skin blanket just big enough for him to look through.

After Little Weasel seemed to be asleep, Older Sister moved over near the fire.

"Skinny little brother," she whispered, "are you asleep yet?"

Little Weasel said nothing, but pretended to sleep.

Older Sister poked the fire with a stick. "Look out," she whispered, "the sparks will burn you."

One of the sparks flew right through the hole in his blanket and burned his cheek, but Little Weasel said nothing and did not move.

"Good," Older Sister said, "he is asleep. Now I can eat." Then, as Little Weasel watched through the hole in his blanket, Older Sister brushed the thick, tangled hair away from her face. Her face was not a human face at all. It was the face of a Keewahkwee, a cannibal monster. She had round red eyes and a wide mouth with many sharp teeth. Blood dripped from her mouth, for she had chewed away her own lips. She reached out her hand to pick up one of the animals that Little Weasel caught. Then she began to eat it raw—skin, bones, and all.

Under his blanket, Little Weasel watched. Older Sister finished eating, and then she looked at the shape of Little Weasel under his blanket.

"He is still bony and thin," she snarled, "but I will not waste any more time fattening him up. I will eat him tomorrow night." Then she turned and curled up in her corner of the cave and slept.

The next morning Older Sister, the Kee-wahkwee, did not ask Little Weasel to allow her to feel his arm.

"Ah," Little Weasel thought. "It is as she said last night. She intends to eat me when I come back."

"Older Sister," Little Weasel said, "I need new moccasins with very strong soles. The ones I am wearing have worn out."

Older Sister grumbled, but she did as he

asked and threw the new moccasins over her shoulder to him.

"Here," she said, "these will last you for as long as you need them."

Little Weasel put on the new moccasins and went out of the cave. He was ready to run away but uncertain which way to go. The rabbit, though, was waiting for him in the forest.

"Do not take the trail you always take. Take the path toward the sunrise," the rabbit said. "Your grandfather lives there, and he will help you."

Little Weasel ran along the path toward the sunrise. Looking out of the cave, Older Sister saw that the boy was not taking the trail that led to his snares.

"What is he doing?" she snarled. She lifted up his deerskin blanket. When she did so, the stick that he had held out to her instead of his arm fell out and she saw the hole in the blanket. "He is running away!" the Keewahkwee cried.

As Little Weasel ran, he suddenly heard a

terrible howl behind him. He knew that the Keewahkwee was chasing him. He ran as hard as he could until he came to another cave in the hillside above him. In the mouth of that cave sat a huge old porcupine.

"My elder," Little Weasel said, "your quills are very clean and beautiful."

"Thank you," said Porcupine. "It is good to meet a young one who is so polite."

"May I hide in your cave?" said Little Weasel. "Keewahkwee is after me."

"Come inside, young one," said Porcupine as he moved aside to let Little Weasel in.

Soon Older Sister, the Keewahkwee, arrived at the mouth of Porcupine's cave.

"Where is the one I am going to eat?" she snarled.

"How do you like my quills?" Porcupine said.

"They are dirty and ugly," Older Sister growled.

"Ah," said Porcupine, "I understand. The one you want to eat is behind me in my cave. You must pass me to get him."

Older Sister, the Keewahkwee, jumped up to enter Porcupine's cave. But as she did so, Porcupine struck her with his quills and killed her.

"Young one," Porcupine said to Little Weasel, "I have killed her, but she will come back to life again. Keep running toward the sunrise to find your grandfather."

Again Little Weasel ran and ran. Soon he reached a wide, swift river with rocky rapids. There a very tall heron stood. Just as he reached the river, he heard the howl of the Keewahkwee, who had come back to life and was on his trail. Little Weasel ran up to Heron.

"My elder," Little Weasel said, "your legs are very long and beautiful."

"Ah-hah," said Heron, "it is good to meet a little one who is so respectful of his elders. Can I help you, little one?"

"Will you help me cross the river?" said Little Weasel. "Keewahkwee is after me."

"Use my leg as a bridge, little one," said Heron as he stretched his long leg across the river to let Little Weasel cross.

Soon Older Sister, the Kee- wahkwee, arrived at the river where Heron stood.

"Where is the one I am going to eat?" she snarled.

"How do you like my legs?" Heron said.

"They are short and ugly," Older Sister growled.

"Ah-hah," said Heron, "I see. The one you want to eat is on the other side. To cross over you must use my leg as a bridge."

Then Heron stretched his long leg across the wide, swift river. Older Sister, the Kee- wahkwee, began to cross. When she was half-way across, Heron shook his leg, and she was thrown into the river, where she was drowned.

"Run, little one," Heron called over to Little Weasel. "The Keewahkwee has drowned, but she will come back to life again. Run toward the sunrise. Your grandfather is there waiting for you."

Once again, Little Weasel ran. He heard the howl of the Keewahkwee behind him, and he ran faster. There, in a broad meadow just ahead of him, next to the ocean, was a big wigwam. An old man with white hair and two tall feathers on his head sat there. The old man had one dark eye and one light eye. By his side sat a tiny dog, no bigger than Little Weasel's hand.

As soon as the dog saw Little Weasel, he ran up, wagging his tail.

"Grandson," the old man said in a happy voice. "You have found your way home. I am glad to see you."

"Grandfather," Little Weasel said, "I am glad to see you, too."

Just then Older Sister, the Keewahkwee, ran into the meadow.

"Now I have caught you," she snarled. "I will eat you and the old man, too."

The old man with white hair smiled. "First," he said, "you must meet my dog." He turned to the tiny dog. "Little Dog," he said, "go and meet this one who wants to eat us."

Little Dog shook himself four times. Each time he shook himself he grew larger and larger, until he was four times as big as the biggest bear. He jumped on the Keewahkwee and chewed her up into bits and ate her. This time she did not come back to life again.

And Little Weasel lived happily with his grandfather and their dog from that day on. When last we saw them, they were living there still.

KEEWAHKWEE (PENOBSCOT)

The story of the cannibal ogre who hides its face from the child it had stolen to fatten up can be found throughout Algonquin traditions. Unlike the giants, who are visibly not human beings, these creatures can pass for people as long as their hideous faces are not seen. The rabbit or some other game animal whose life is spared and who then helps a child is a common theme in such stories. By behav-

ing politely to his elders (animal or human), while the cannibal ogre is always rude, the little boy or girl is able to
escape his pursuer and find the way back to his or her real
family.

Sources:

"Penobscot Tales and Religious Beliefs," by Frank G.
    Speck, *Journal of American Folklore* (1935).

The Algonquin Legends of New England, by Charles G. Leland
    (Boston: Houghton and Mifflin, 1884).

YAKWAWIAK

Of all the creatures that walked the earth on four legs, the Yakwawiak* were the largest. The earth shook under their feet, and the other animals ran from them, for these monsters were bad-tempered and unfriendly. The human beings had been given permission by Kitselemukong, the Great Mystery, to hunt the animals for food. But they too were afraid of the Yakwawiak.

The skin and the hair of the Yakwawiak were so thick that no arrow could pierce them. The two great tusks of these monsters were as

*In Algonquin languages, plural forms are made with a "k," not an "s." Yakwawiak is plural, Yakwawi is singular.

sharp as spears, and their long noses were like great snakes. The Yakwawiak hurled down the trees and muddied the springs. They trampled everything underfoot as they went about the land. They crushed the humans and the animals under their feet, and the people had to hide in caves to escape them. Those great monsters did not remember the words of Kitselemukong, who said that all beings on earth should live together. The Yakwawiak had no respect for any other living thing.

At last, one man could take it no longer. This man, whose name was Two Hawks Flying, left the caves where all the people were hiding from the great monsters. He climbed to the top of the highest mountain. He made a fire and prayed to the Creator. He placed tobacco on the glowing coals. As the smoke rose up into the sky, he spoke his words to Kitselemukong.

"Great Mystery," Two Hawks Flying said, "you are the one who made all things. You are the one who said that we should all live together and respect each other. But the Yakwawiak have forgotten your words. They wish to kill all of the other beings in the world. Help us, Creator, or we will all be destroyed."

Kitselemukong saw that this could not continue and decided to take pity on the people.

A great light appeared in front of Two Hawks Flying.

"Hear me," said a voice from within that light, which was Kitselemukong. "I will help you. Call all of the people and the animals together. Have them gather here at dawn."

"I will do as you say," said Two Hawks Flying.

Then he went to speak to the people and all of the other animals.

"Kitselemukong has told me that all of us must come together in council," Two Hawks Flying said. Everyone who heard him, both the humans and the animals, knew that his words were true, and they began to gather.

The wolf and the bear, the moose and the mountain lion, the lynx and the wolverine, the elk and deer and all of the other animals, including many whose names are now forgotten, came together. The human beings came from their hiding places in the caves and joined them. They all gathered on the mountaintop where Two Hawks Flying had prayed.

"You must drive the Yakwawiak from the land," the voice of Kitselemukong said from within that great glowing light. "They have forgotten to respect other beings. Now you must all join together and make war on them."

So the people and all of the animals began to make war on the Yakwawiak. Side by side, they marched together toward the Yakwawiak, but the Yakwawiak were waiting. The earth shook under their feet as they charged, and the fight began.

Kitselemukong watched from the top of the highest mountain as they fought. It was a hard battle, for the Yakwawiak were strong. The Yakwawiak tried to crush the animals and people beneath their huge feet. They stabbed them with their sharp tusks and threw them up into the air with their trunks. The piercing sound of their screams as they fought was terrible to hear. Even when they were wounded and bleeding, the huge monsters continued to fight.

All through that long day, the fight went back and forth. It went from the edge of the great salt water to the wide river that flows through the heart of the land. Many of the bravest animals, those who were almost as large and powerful as the Yakwawiak, were killed. The giant bear and the great wolf fell, and the huge beaver fell in battle. Only their bones buried in the earth show that they ever lived. Many of the people and the other animals were also killed in the fight, but they still fought bravely. One of the bravest was Two Hawks Flying.

The air was filled with the terrible screams of the Yakwawiak as they fought. Mountains were pushed over and valleys gouged out by the monsters as they fought. The earth sank down and became marshy as it was trampled under the feet of the huge creatures. Blood soaked into the ground.

But Two Hawks Flying saw that the Yakwawiak were too powerful. The human beings and the animals could not defeat them alone.

"Great One," he shouted, "you must help us now."

So Kitselemukong began to hurl down lightning from the top of the highest mountain. Each time a bolt of lightning struck, one of the Yakwawiak was killed. Finally, only the largest of the terrible monsters remained. He was so large that the other monsters seemed small in comparison. It seemed that nothing could defeat him. Each time a lightning bolt was hurled at him, he knocked it away with his tusks. But this one Yakwawi had been wounded many times, and he was growing weaker. At last he turned and began to run. He ran toward the cold north land, where no trees grow and there is always ice and snow. Some tried to follow him, but Two Hawks Flying called them back.

"No," he said. "That one is the last of his kind. He will no longer bother us."

Some say that Yakwawi is still hiding there to this day. You may hear his awful cry in the howl of the north wind. Sometimes, it is said, a lone hunter may chance upon the Yakwawi in that far northern land. If that hunter has not been a good man, if he has killed animals needlessly and not shared with others, such a hunter never returns to his people.

When we dig into the earth in the places where that battle raged long ago, we find the bones and the giant tusks of the Yakwawiak. Nothing else remains of them in the lands of the Lenape, the human beings.

But Kitselemukong left one other sign on the earth of that great battle. In the marsh-lands created by that long-ago fight, there where the blood soaked into the earth, Kitselemukong made a new berry grow. Its skin is as red as the blood that was shed. It is the cranberry. When the people see it, they remember  the fate of the Yakwawiak, those great crea-tures who had no respect for the rest of the creation.

YAKWAWIAK (LENAPE)

The mastodon, although it has supposedly been extinct for ten thousand years, is still found in a surprisingly large number of the traditions of the Native Americans of the Northeast—from the Abenaki to the Iroquois to the Lenape. Either the oral traditions have a very long memory, or these elephant-like creatures survived much longer than paleontologists believe. Called the "stiff-legged bear" or the "walking hill" in some Native languages, the mastodon or mammoth was apparently a very fearsome being to the Lenape and other Native people who saw it walk the earth that shook beneath its feet.

Sources:

The Algonquin Legends of New England, by Charles G. Leland (Boston: Houghton and Mifflin, 1884).

Folk Medicine of the Delaware, by Gladys Tantaquidgeon, Pennsylvania Historical and Museum Commission Anthropological Series (1972).

The White Deer and Other Stories Told by the Lenape, by John Bierhorst (New York: William Morrow and Company, Inc., 1995).

The Grandfathers Speak: Native American Folk Tales of the Lenape People, by Hitakonanu'laxk (Interlink Books, 1994).

MAN BEAR

Swift Runner raised his hands over his head and looked back. The other young men had not yet completed half of the race, but he had already circled the village and reached the great standing stone that stood in the center of the village and was the symbol of his people.

"Wah-hey!" he shouted. "I am Aiyanno-weh, Swift Runner. I am truly the fastest runner of all. No one on two legs or four legs can defeat me!"

As the people gathered around to congratulate him, Swift Runner's father shook his head.

"I am worried," Burden Carrier said. "My son brags too much."

Swift Runner's grandmother smiled. "It is true that he speaks loudly," White Hummingbird said. "But he has a good heart. After all, the young always like to boast about the things they do. And he only speaks the truth."

Burden Carrier could not disagree. There was no one who had ever been able to run as swiftly as his younger son. He was so fast a runner that he no longer hunted with a bow. Now, whenever he hunted, he would simply chase the animal he was after until it fell from exhaustion. The deer, the elk, and the buffalo were unable to outrun him. He watched as Swift Runner waited to congratulate the other young men who finished the race after him. As each one reached the standing stone, Swift Runner clasped their hands.

"You have run well," Swift Runner said to each exhausted young man. "Do not be ashamed. No one can defeat me, for I am Swift Runner."

Burden Carrier shook his head again. "I

remember what happened to his older brother, and I worry about my remaining son."

White Hummingbird placed her hand on Burden Carrier's shoulder. Swift Runner's older brother, Quick Feet, had boasted that he could outrun a whole herd of deer in a single day. Quick Feet ran all through the day without resting, racing one deer after another until they fell from exhaustion. But just as the sun was about to set, Quick Feet himself fell. His heart had burst.

"Do not worry," White Hummingbird said. "You have taught your younger son well."

"That may be so," Burden Carrier said, "but strange things are happening now. Some of the best hunters have gone out and never returned. Others have come back saying that they saw the tracks of a man that ended where the tracks of a great bear began. It may be that a Man Bear is now hunting our people. What if such a powerful being hears my son's words and challenges him?"

"Then he will do his best," White Hummingbird said.

That night, as the people gathered around the central fire inside their great longhouse, they heard a voice call from outside.

"Swift Runner," the voice growled, "I have come to speak to you."

Then a man stepped through the open door. He was taller and broader than any man the people had seen before. He wore the skin of a huge bear around his shoulders. Two long, sharp bear teeth hung from the necklace that he wore. His eyes glowed red as he stared at the people.

Swift Runner stood to face the man.

"I am Swift Runner," he said. "No one on two legs or four legs can defeat me."

"Hunh," the Man Bear growled. "None of your people have escaped me so far. I have come to challenge you to race me."

"I accept your challenge," said Swift Runner.

"We will race tomorrow," the Man Bear rumbled, his great voice shaking the walls of the longhouse. "We'll run from dawn until sunset. At sunset the one who loses will die."

Then he turned and went out the door.

Burden Carrier and White Hummingbird took Swift Runner aside as the people within the longhouse talked in hushed voices about the terrible being who had just visited them. Many feared that if Swift Runner lost, the Man Bear would destroy them all.

"My son," Burden Carrier said, "it will not be easy to defeat a Man Bear. Do not exhaust yourself chasing him. Remember that he will try to trick you."

"I will remember what you taught me, Father," Swift Runner said.

White Hummingbird reached into the pouch at her side and took out two small feathers. She held them out to her grandson.

"The hummingbird is the smallest of the birds, but the swiftest," she said. "Carry these feathers with you in  the pouch around your neck, and they will make your feet even faster." Then she handed her grandson a small blowgun with a sharp wooden dart feathered with cattail down. "There is only one place where the Man Bear can be killed," she said to him. She leaned close to her grandson's ear. "I will whisper it to you."

At dawn, Swift Runner stepped outside the longhouse. Still in the shape of a human being, the Man Bear was waiting.

"Now you will run," the Man Bear growled, "and I will chase you."

Swift Runner grasped the pouch that hung around his neck. "No," he said, "you will run, and I will chase *you*."

Swift Runner's words surprised the Man Bear, for they were his own magic words turned back on him. The Man Bear began to run and soon was out of sight.

"Run as fast as you can," Swift Runner shouted, "but you cannot escape me."

Then Swift Runner began to follow the tracks of the Man Bear. Soon the human tracks turned into those of a giant bear. The trail was easy to follow, for the Man Bear knocked over trees as he ran, and his feet tore great gouges in the earth.

Swift Runner reached the top of a hill and looked down through the valley below. He could see the Man Bear running on four legs ahead of him.

"I can catch him now," Swift Runner said to himself, "but I must remember what my father told me. He will try to trick me by hiding at the end of that valley where he can jump out and attack me. So I will not go that way."

Then Swift Runner made a great circle to go around the valley. He climbed a hill and looked down. Sure enough, the Man Bear was crouched behind a tall pine at the end of the valley, waiting to leap out.

"Ah-hoo!" Swift Runner called down to the Man Bear.

The Man Bear looked up at him in surprise.

"Are you tired?" Swift Runner shouted. "Start running now, or I will catch you!"

With an angry roar, the Man Bear began

to run even faster than before. But Swift Runner did not follow right away.

"I must remember what my father told me," Swift Runner said. "I must not exhaust myself." Then he sat down and took some food from the pouch at his side. He drank water from a nearby stream and ate. When he was rested, he began to follow the trail of the Man Bear again. The sun was in the middle of the sky, and the Man Bear had gotten far ahead, but Swift Runner's long strides carried him quickly along the trail. Finally he could see the Man Bear running ahead of him.

"You cannot escape me," Swift Runner shouted. "I am close behind you."

Hearing those magic words, the Man Bear  ran even faster until, once again, it went out of sight.

"I could catch him now," Swift Runner said, "but I must remember my father's words. I will rest again."

Once more, Swift Runner rested as his

father had told him to do. He drank water and ate a little food and felt refreshed. Then, just as before, he ran and caught up with the Man Bear.

By now, the sun was getting low in the sky. Swift Runner stayed close behind the monster bear, not getting close enough so that it could strike at him. The Man Bear was growing tired. Its sides puffed in and out as it ran, and it groaned now with each stride.

"Run faster," Swift Runner shouted, "I am after you."

But the Man Bear could run no faster. It could run no farther. Just as the sun began to set, it fell to the ground with exhaustion, and Swift Runner ran past it.

"I have defeated you," Swift Runner said. "Now you must die."

The monster bear lay panting on its side, but it looked at him with crafty eyes.

"Come close and try to kill me," it growled. "If you fail to kill me with your first blow, then I will destroy you."

But Swift Runner kept his distance. He

unslung the blowgun from around his neck and lifted it to his mouth. "I know the one place where you are weak," Swift Runner said. Then he shot the sharp dart straight into the Man Bear's foot, where its heart was hidden, and the monster died.

Swift Runner pulled out the two great teeth of the Man Bear and hung them around his own neck. He took the trail that led back to the village. Although it had taken him a single day to run this far, it took him four days to get back home.

All the people praised him for saving them from the Man Bear.

"I am proud of you," said Burden Carrier as he embraced his son. "Now you may brag all that you wish. Truly no one on two legs or four·legs can defeat you."

But Swift Runner shook his head. "I have no need to brag any further," he said.

And from that day on, even though everyone else remembered his great deed and spoke of it, Swift Runner was the most modest of all men.

MAN BEAR (ONEIDA)

Tales of shape-shifting monsters remain common to this day among the Oneida and the other Iroquois people. We have heard not only tales of were-bears, but also, these days, of people who turn into cats, dogs, and even pigs to do evil deeds. The Man Bear, which is able to change back into a man and hunts human beings, is one of the most fearsome of the monsters of the deep woods. Some say that the Man Bear is based on the grizzly bear, a fearlessly dangerous animal that may have now and then found its way onto Iroquois lands. A grizzly bear is very hard to kill with arrows or spears. Many Native American monsters, like the Man Bear, hide their hearts in some unexpected place so that no one can kill them unless they know the secret.

Sources:

Iroquois Folk Lore, by William M. Beauchamp (Port Washington, N.Y.: Kennikat Press, 1965; reissue of 1922 edition).

Legends of the Longhouse, by Jesse J. Cornplanter (Port Washington, N.Y.: Kennikat Press, 1938).

Seneca Myths and Folk Tales, by Arthur C. Parker (Buffalo, N.Y.: Buffalo Historical Society, 1923).

THE SPREADERS

It was the Moon of Moose Hunting in the year the Awanootsak, the white men, called 1750. Floating single file down the wide Kwanitewk, Pitolo and Azon had paddled their heavily laden canoes for most of the day. The two Abenaki men were headed for the English settlements to trade their furs.

"We should pull over and make camp," Azone said, looking toward the setting sun.

"Not here, let's just go a little bit farther," Pitolo answered, scanning the thickly wooded forest surrounding them.

"Pretty soon it will be dark. We have all

day tomorrow to finish this journey," Azone insisted. He pulled alongside Pitolo's canoe.

"When I was a young boy, my grandfather took me on this stretch of river. He told me never to camp along these shores. Just another mile, and then we can camp," Pitolo responded, continuing to paddle at a steady pace.

"Sounds like more of your grandfather's superstitions. What is it now, Man Bears?"

"No, Spreaders," Pitolo said in a very serious tone.

"What are Spreaders?" asked Azone.

"Little People. Very mean Little People."

"Why would you be scared of little people?"

"My grandfather never really told me that much about them. They are as small as little children, with arms and legs as skinny as sticks. But they are very strong and bad-tempered. Even the big bears are afraid of them. If any animal tries to bite them, they shove sticks into its mouth so that its mouth is wedged open. They like to spread things open with sticks. Grandfather warned me never to camp in their territory. And if I remember correctly, this is it," Pitolo answered, continuing to paddle.

"Nonsense, that is nothing but a childhood story. I refuse to paddle anymore, I'm pulling over here. If you want to camp farther down, go ahead," Azone said in a disgusted voice.

Pulling up on shore, Azone jumped out of his canoe and began unloading his gear. After pausing for a moment, Pitolo shook his head and then resumed his paddling, heading farther downriver. He said nothing. He knew that once Azone made up his mind, no one could convince him to do otherwise.

"I'll meet you downstream in the morning!" Azone shouted toward Pitolo's back. Then he began to set up his camp.

Pitolo paddled faster. It would be dark soon, leaving him little time to set up his own camp. Childish or not, true or untrue, Pitolo had always honored what his elders told him. No matter what, he wasn't going to risk camping along that shoreline.

Two hours later darkness had set in. A mile downriver, Pitolo had set up his camp. Sitting around his small fire drinking a cup of pine needle tea, he thought about Azone. Although he too wondered if the story was true, he couldn't help but worry about his friend. After finishing his tea, Pitolo walked over to the water's edge. Having camped on a peninsula, looking upstream, he could just barely make out the light from Azone's fire. Satisfied his friend was well, Pitolo walked back toward his own fire and lay down for the night.

Meanwhile, at Azone's camp, Azone was already sleeping soundly. Convinced Pitolo's fears were completely unfounded, Azone had wrapped himself in his blanket shortly after making his fire. Such a deep sleep it was, having paddled all day, that at first he wasn't awakened by the soft sounds of many small feet quietly moving closer and closer. Closer and closer.

After packing his canoe the next morning, Pitolo waited by the shore for Azone. He expected to see him paddling along any minute.

The sun continued to climb higher in the sky. By the time it was four hands high, Pitolo began to worry. He paddled back up the river toward Azone's camp. Once close enough, he shouted for his friend.

"Azone! Azone, where are you?" There was no response. Truly worried now, Pitolo pulled up on the shore and stepped out of his canoe.

"Azone!" Still there was no response. He walked around looking carefully. There was no sign of Azone or his canoe. Instead, he found a neatly put out fire and little trace that anyone had ever camped there.

Pitolo smiled. "Ah, that Azone. He has left without me. He got up before dawn and slipped by me while I was still asleep! He is trying to beat me to the settlements!" Pitolo jumped back into his canoe and began to paddle down the river, without looking over the small rise just beyond Azone's camp.

There, hidden from sight only fifty feet away, still filled with furs, lay Azone's canoe. Next to it was another canoe, and another next to that. Many canoes lay there—Abenaki, Mahican, Mohawk, English, and French canoes. All were in varying stages of decay, some having completely returned to the earth. A little farther back in the woods, near the dry skeletons and scattered bones of many men, lay Azone.

Wakened in the middle of the night, he had tried to run. But something had hit his head. Regaining consciousness early that morning, he had found himself there. Twigs were placed between all his toes and fingers, spreading them out as far as they could go. Sticks spread his arms and legs out so wide he couldn't move. Twigs propped his eyes and mouth wide open.

Hearing Pitolo calling for him, he had tried to respond. But his mouth was so dry that all that came out were low moans. They were too low for Pitolo to have heard, just as he was too far away to have been seen. As his friend disappeared down the long river, all Azone could do was wait. His fate would be the same as all those before him who dared to bother the Spreaders by camping on their shores.

Pitolo reached the settlement downriver and waited for his friend. But Azone never arrived. Although Pitolo looked for his friend and asked others in the settlement about him, his search was in vain. At last Pitolo sadly decided that Azone had become another of those who bothered the Spreaders and would never be seen again.

THE SPREADERS (ABENAKI)

The Abenaki say there are many different kinds of Little People. Some take care of the forest creatures, making sure that people do not do things that would be destructive—such as gathering too many plants or hunting too many animals. Other Little People watch over the gardens or listen in to make sure that humans are not telling stories at the wrong season. The Spreaders are Little People who live along certain rivers—for example, one very dangerous stretch of the St. Maurice in Quebec. When you invade their territory by sleeping overnight next to their places by the river, you may wake up with sticks stuck between your fingers and toes, your arms and legs, and your eyes and mouth propped open. If you are unlucky, no one will find you, and you will not survive. The Little People must always be treated with great respect.

Sources:

Unpublished oral tradition: told by Abenaki elders Maurice Dennis, Stephen Laurent, and Cecile Wawanolett.

The Original Vermonters, by William Haviland and Margery Powers (University Presses of New England, 1981).

AGLEBEMU

You can't have it. It's mine," Louis said as
he wrestled the ball out of his little
brother Allen's hand.

Allen looked at Louis with sad eyes.

"We're supposed to share," he said.

Louis shook his head. "Not this," he said.
"This is mine." He tilted his head toward the
river that flowed around their island. "You almost let it roll into the water. You would have
lost it."

"But I didn't," Allen said. "I didn't." He
looked like he was about to cry.

For a moment, Louis almost gave in. Then
he thought of how long he had waited to have

a ball like this. He held it up, seeing how beautiful its white cowhide surface was and admiring the neat hand-sewn stitches. It was the first real baseball to be brought to the island. It had been given to Father by a tall white man whose carriage was pulled by a beautiful roan mare. He had bought one of Father's carved canes and then given him that ball. Father had brought it back to the island.

"Someday," Father had said, "maybe you will be really good at baseball."

Then he had placed it in Louis's hand. Louis held tighter to the ball as he remembered his father's words.

"No," Louis said. "This ball is mine. Father gave it to me."

"Aglebemu," said a voice from behind him.

Startled, Louis turned around and saw Uncle John Bear. He knew more of the old stories than anyone else on Indian Island. The children all loved to listen to those stories that he would only tell when the snow covered the ground and people gathered around the fire.

Uncle John reached out one of his long,

gnarled fingers and gently tapped Louis on the chest. "Aglebemu," he said again.

"No," Louis whispered, holding tighter to the ball.

"Unh-hunh," said Uncle John. His deep-set eyes looked straight at Louis. "Aglebemu."

Louis turned and ran as fast as he could, leaving his little brother and the old man behind. He ran around the bend and along the shore of the island until he came to a small boat that was pulled partway up onto the beach. It was his Aunt Molly's boat. He climbed in and ducked down. No one would find him here.

"I am not Aglebemu," he whispered. "I am not."

He closed his eyes and leaned back. It wasn't right for Uncle John to call him that. But that name and the story connected to it kept going through his mind. He could hear Uncle John's voice as he told the story five months ago, when the January ice was thick on the river and the howling voice of North Wind rattled the windows.

Long ago, Uncle John had said, there was a great monster known as Aglebemu. He was as tall as a big pine tree. He had a fat, green body and a big head with huge eyes and a mouth large enough to swallow a bull moose. His fingers were as long and yellow as the roots of a birch tree. He lived in the waters of our river. He wanted all the water for himself.

So Aglebemu made a great dam upstream. The river dried up. The fish and other water creatures died. Even the little spirits that live in the river and help the people began to die. But Aglebemu did not care. He wanted the water for himself. He got into that water, and he swallowed some of it and floated around in the rest of it. When the people downstream begged for water, he said he could not give them any. It all belonged to Aglebemu, and he kept chanting his name.

Aglebemu, Aglebemu, Aglebemu.

People tried to fight him, but Aglebemu was so huge that he just opened his big mouth and swallowed them up.

Gluskabe the changer, the one the Creator

made to help the human beings, finally had to come. First he fought with Aglebemu. Then he poked a hole in Aglebemu's stomach with his spear, and all the water rushed out. He broke Aglebemu's dam. Then he squeezed Aglebemu and made him very small. He changed him into a bullfrog. In the summer nights you can still hear him saying his name. Aglebemu, Aglebemu, Aglebemu.

Uncle John Bear had paused then and looked around at the circle of children listening to him.

"I think maybe," Uncle John said, "Aglebemu has gotten bigger again after all these years. You see how some people now don't want to share anything. They want to own everything."

As Louis remembered that story, he curled up on his side. It was warm inside the boat, and it rocked gently in the water. Louis had not noticed it, but when he climbed in he had pushed the boat into the water, and now it was floating slowly out into the river. Louis closed his eyes.

When he opened them again, it was dark.

He sat up and looked around. Where was the shore? There were no lights to be seen anywhere. The boat had drifted downstream, and he did not know where he was. He felt inside the boat for the oars. Then he remembered that he had not seen them. Aunt Molly must have taken them with her. A boat with oars in it was a boat that anyone could borrow. Taking out the oars meant that someone planned to use that boat again soon.

Louis put his hand in the water. It was warm and still. That meant he had drifted into a backwater out of the main flow of the Penobscot River. It would be harder for anyone to find him until it was light again. But did anyone know where he was? His heart began to beat so hard that he could hear it pounding. He tried to calm himself down. "There's no reason to be afraid," he whispered.

He sat back, thinking he would try to sleep again.

AGLE-BE-MUUUUUU!

The sound was so loud that it made him jump up. He almost fell out of the boat.

AGLE-BE-MUUUUUU!

He had heard bullfrogs before, but never one this loud. Maybe it was true what Uncle John said. Maybe Aglebemu had become a giant again. Maybe Aglebemu was going to come and get him because he had been so selfish. It was true. He knew it now. He had acted just like Aglebemu.

Something splashed in the water nearby. He looked over the side of the boat. He could see a big head in the water. It was slowly coming toward him. Perhaps it was only a beaver. But then the moonlight glinted from its big eyes.

AGLE-BE-MUUUUUU! AGLE-BE-MUUUUUU! AGLE-BE-MUUUUUU!

Louis shrank back into the boat and closed his eyes. Had it seen him? Something brushed against the boat, and the boat began to rock. Louis looked up. He thought he could see a big green hand with fingers as long as tree roots reaching up over the end of the boat.

The air shook from the sound of the huge bullfrog's voice.

AGLE-BE-MUUUUU! AGLE-BE-MUUUUU! AGLE-BE-MUUUUU!

"I'm sorry," Louis shouted at the top of his lungs. "I'm sorry! I'm sorry! I'm sorry!"

Suddenly, the bullfrog's sound stopped. The hand, if it had ever been there, was gone. Louis sat up. He could hear a distant voice drifting over the water. The voice was calling his name.

"Louissss." He knew that voice. It was his father.

"Louisss," a smaller voice called. Allen.

"I am here," Louis shouted back. A small point of light appeared, coming from around a point of land that he had not been able to see before in the dark. It was a torch in the front of another boat. Allen held that torch as their father rowed.

"Did you see that?" Allen said, his voice excited. "There was something really big next to your boat, Louis."

"I'm glad you found me," Louis said.

Soon he had climbed in with them, and they had tied Aunt Molly's boat onto the back of theirs. Louis sat down next to Allen in front of their father as he began to row back up the river.

Behind them, the bullfrog's voice again began to fill the night.

"Aglebemu is pretty loud tonight," Father said. "Sounds like he still wants it all himself." He looked down at the baseball that Louis still held in his hand.

Allen reached out a hand and patted Louis on his leg.

"I saw you get into Aunt Molly's boat," Allen said. "But I didn't want to bother you. When I came back later and saw the boat was gone, I told Father." Allen paused and looked at Louis. "Did I do good?"

Louis looked down at the baseball that he still held in one hand. He held it out to his brother. "I know you won't lose it," he said.

AGLEBEMU (PENOBSCOT)
Aglebemu is one of the many monsters that were defeated and transformed by Gluskabe, the changer hero of Wabanaki culture. When the water of the world is held back by

the great frog, who builds a huge dam, Gluskabe must go and break that dam to release the waters to the thirsty people. Aglebemu's name is also the sound that a frog makes. On summer nights you can still hear his big selfish voice saying, "I will give them none."

Sources
"Penobscot Tales and Religious Beliefs," by Frank G.
   Speck, *Journal of American Folklore*, January–March
   1935.

BIG TREE PEOPLE

It's your turn to look out for Dad," Lloyd Little Deer said, poking his head out from under the covers of the bed.

"No, it's your turn," Aaron Little Deer said. Lately Aaron always said that it wasn't his turn. He was four years old and had recently decided he was too old for his brothers and sisters to tell him what to do.

"Shhh!" Mary said from the bed across from theirs.

She and Sarah and Tammy slept there. Their double bed was the one that all five of them played on when they were supposed to be sleeping. Phil and Aaron and Lloyd's bed was not any smaller, but it was too creaky.

Lloyd swung his bare feet out and placed them on the cool floorboards of the little attic room where they slept. The big window just over their bed was filled with the light of the full moon. The branches of the nearby trees swayed in the wind.

It was November — Frost Moon, as the old people called it. There were no leaves on the trees, and the tips of the branches scraped at the windows. A little shiver went down Lloyd's back. Those twigs almost looked like bony fingers. It made Lloyd think of some of the scary stories that Dad told about monsters. In the dark outside it was easy to imagine a hungry Flying Head howling through the air or a big Stone Giant hiding behind one of the houses. Lloyd shivered again and looked away from the window.

"Listen," Lloyd said, "we all agreed we would take turns. Last night was Phil's turn."

Phil nodded. It was his belief that few words were good, and no words at all even better. He was the best listener of all the Little Deer children. He was also the best of all at looking out for Dad. By having one of them be the lookout, they were always able to trick Dad whenever he came up to see if they were playing after it was time to be quiet. They would have plenty of time to get back into their beds, pull up the covers, and pretend to sleep. So far, Dad had never been able to catch them.

When Phil was the lookout, they always had the most warning. He could hear Dad coming even before Dad's feet were on the long staircase to the attic. Phil's brothers and sisters tried to make that his permanent job. Phil just shook his head and said no. Each night one of them had to take a turn at lookout. Tonight was Aaron's turn.

Everyone looked at Aaron, who sat with his arms folded and his lips sticking out.

"Please," Mary and Sarah said.

"Pretty please," said Lloyd.

"Double pretty please," Tammy said.

Phil just looked at Aaron and said nothing.

Aaron looked around at them all. Then he smiled. "Okay," he said. He got up, wrapped a blanket around his shoulders, tiptoed over to the head of the stairs, and looked down. He turned back and bobbed his hand up and down. "All clear," he whispered.

Lloyd jumped up onto the bed with a pillow in his hand. He threw it back at Phil. Soon they were all playing, jumping up and down on the bed, throwing pillows. Mary grabbed Lloyd's leg, and Lloyd fell on his back. Phil grabbed one of his arms, and Sarah grabbed the other. Then Tammy and Aaron started tickling him. He tried not to laugh too loud. But how could Aaron be tickling him? Aaron was supposed to be on lookout duty at the head of the stairs!

"HAAA-RUUMPPHHH!"

The loud sound of an adult clearing his throat made them all stop what they were doing. Six sets of eyes turned toward the head of the stairs. Harold Little Deer, their father, stood there, his arms folded over his chest.

Lloyd waited for Dad to scold them. Then

he noticed something strange. Dad wasn't looking at them. He was staring at the window.

"I think I saw one of them," he said. "Just outside your window." His voice was very serious.

"One of who, Dad?" Mary and Sarah said.

"You don't want to know," Dad said. "I just hope it didn't see you."

Lloyd couldn't stand it any longer. "What are you talking about, Dad?"

Harold Little Deer turned and looked at him. Then he shook his head. "The Big Tree People, son. That's who I'm talking about. Around this time of year they come down from the hills and head into town. They look like big trees, but they're really hungry giants. They have long arms like branches and skinny fingers like twigs. They look into the upstairs windows—just like that one there over your bed—to see if they can see any children. That's what they eat, you know, little children. If you lie real still in bed, they don't notice you. They tap against the windows then, like a branch being swayed by the wind. *Tack-tacck. Tack-tacck. Tack-tacck.*

"If you sit up and move around, they will see you for sure. And if they do, they *reach right in through the window and grab you.*"

Harold Little Deer sighed. "It's too bad, you know. Once they grab a child, there's nothing anyone can do about it. Some people say they tear the children up into little pieces. Others say they just swallow them whole. Sometimes people find bones here and there around the rez. They are so gnawed up, no one knows where those bones come from. Maybe they're from those kids who get grabbed. All that we know for sure is that once a Big Tree Person gets someone, they're never seen again."

Lloyd swallowed hard and looked over at Phil. They both remembered the chewed-up bones that he and Phil had found by the creek. The older kids had said they were just pig bones.

Harold Little Deer looked out the window. "Was that tree there before? It just doesn't look familiar to me. Hmm. Do you kids think that might be one of them?"

Harold Little Deer turned back and looked around at the children, who had all slowly climbed into bed as he talked. "Well, I got to go back downstairs now. Sleep good, kids."

The six children listened to the sound of his footsteps going down the stairs.

"Are there really Big Tree People?" Aaron said in a shaky voice.

Lloyd started to answer him, but he didn't get the chance.

Tack-tacck. Tack-tacck. Tack-tacck.

It was the tapping of a tree branch against the big window. Or was it?

"Everybody be quiet and don't move!" Phil whispered. And that was the last thing any of them said.

BIG TREE PEOPLE (ONONDAGA)
The Big Tree People are only one of many different creatures whose mission it is to look out for disobedient chil-

dren and carry them away. In this case, they look like tall leafless trees and stand very still when anyone looks directly at them. They peer into windows late at night to reach in and grab children who are not yet asleep.

Sources:

Unpublished oral tradition: told to us by Mike Tarbell, an Onondaga Indian writer.

TOAD WOMAN

It was late summer. Sozap and his two friends David and Billy quickly finished off their lunch. After thanking Sozap's mother, they headed toward the door.

"Remember to stay away from the cedar bog," Sozap's mother reminded the three boys as they went out the door.

"Yes, Mother!" Sozap called back from across the front yard.

Sozap, David, and Billy headed for their fort. It was deep in the forest behind Sozap's house. The three boys had been working on their fort all summer and were anxious to complete it. That morning David's father had given them just enough old lumber to finish off their roof.

When they reached the fort, the boys set to work. Climbing up on the roof next to his friend, David turned toward Sozap.

"Why is your mother always so worried about that cedar bog?"

"When I was younger she used to tell my brother and me stories about this . . . monster that lived there," Sozap said, continuing to hammer on a nail.

"What kind of monster?" Billy called up from below them.

"A creature named Toad Woman. My mother said she was a very evil old woman that would lure young children into the bog with her beautiful voice and then drown them," Sozap told the two boys, who had stopped hammering.

Billy climbed up the ladder and sat down on the other side of Sozap.

"Do you believe it?" Billy asked.

"Not really. She used to tell us lots of stories like that. I think she was just worried we might fall in the bog or something."

"So, have you ever been to that bog?" Billy asked.

Sozap paused for a moment before answering. He knew exactly what his friend was leading up to.

"Once, about five years ago. My father took me there."

"What was it like?" David asked.

"I don't remember very much because I was so young, but I do remember I was scared."

"I think we should go there. It sounds really cool." Billy said. His voice was excited.

"I thought you guys wanted to work on the fort." Sozap picked up a nail and went back to his hammering.

"I vote for the cedar bog," David said.

"Me, too," said Billy. "Let's go now."

Sozap looked at his friends. "I don't know. It's pretty far away. It'll be dark soon, and I promised my mother we wouldn't."

"What's the matter? Scared of the toad lady?" Billy began to laugh.

Sozap felt cornered. He didn't want to upset his mother. But he also didn't like being called a chicken.

"So? We going or what?" asked David.

At first Sozap said nothing. This is no time to be scared of childish stories, he thought. After all, I'll be eleven years old in a month. Still, Sozap didn't like the thought of upsetting his mother. Finally, he came to a compromise.

"O.K. We can go to the cedar bog. But first we finish off the roof. And you have to promise not to tell anyone." What his mother didn't know couldn't hurt her.

"We promise," both boys said. They all set to work. In a few hours they had finished the roof.

"Ready?" David said.

Sozap put down his hammer and sighed. "Okay."

Sozap led the two boys through the woods in the direction of the cedar bog. Although he hadn't been there since he was younger, Sozap knew exactly where it was. It was the only part of the forest that his parents considered off limits.

After walking for quite some time, the boys found themselves within a couple of hundred yards of the bog. As they crossed a small meadow, Sozap looked over at the sun. It was sinking lower in the sky. He began to rethink his decision. Even though the story of Toad Woman wasn't true, he felt a knot beginning to form in his stomach.

"Wow, this is pretty cool," said Billy, standing at the edge of the bog.

In front of them, as far as the eye could see, were countless cedar trees. The tops of each tree's roots were just above water, forming hundreds of small green islands. Each island was surrounded by black swampy water filled with cedar needles.

"Check this out!" yelled David. He began jumping from one tree's roots to the next. It wasn't hard to do, for most were only three to four feet apart.

"I don't think that's a good idea, David," Sozap said in a concerned tone.

"Sure it is! Looks like fun to me," answered Billy.

He, too, began jumping from one island to the next. Within a few moments, both boys were far out into the bog. Each of them was heading in a different direction. Sozap, feeling the knot in his stomach grow tighter, remained where he was.

"How far back do you think this bog goes?" Billy yelled to David, who was now at least fifty yards away.

As his friends went deeper and deeper into the bog, Sozap, still standing at the edge of the bog, looked once again toward the western horizon. Through the thick forest, he could just barely make out the rays from the sun slowly slipping behind the mountains.

"Hey, guys. You better come back now! It's going to be dark soon!"

"Just a minute, I think I'm near the other side!" David yelled back.

Even with his hands cupped behind his ears, Sozap barely heard David's response. Both boys were now totally out of his sight.

Billy had stopped when he heard Sozap's shout. But David had continued on.

"Wow, this place is endless. Isn't it, Billy?" he said, after making another huge leap between islands. There was no response. David paused for a moment. "Billy, did you hear me? . . . Where are you?"

David looked around. There was no one there. He had gone much farther into the bog than he'd realized. "Hey, you guys?"

David tried to go back the way he had come. Darkness, however, was setting in. He soon lost track of where he was. His heart was pumping with fear. Sweat began to pour down the side of his face.

"Billy, Sozap! Where are you?" he yelled as loud as he could.

"Over here, David!" It was the voices of Sozap and Billy responding to him from the far edge of the bog. David sighed with relief.

But they were so far away, and it was so much darker. It was hard to judge how far away each of the islands was.

"Keep yelling, so I know where to go!" David shouted. There was a desperate tone in his voice, even though he knew they couldn't be more than a hundred yards away. As he jumped from one small island to the next, David listened for the sound of his friends' voices. But as the last rays of sunlight slowly disappeared, he heard nothing, and each jump became more difficult. David's heart raced faster and faster. More sweat poured down his face. Then, as he paused to catch his breath, he began to hear a strange, sweet sound.

Standing on the shore, Sozap and Billy had been shouting for their friend for at least three minutes straight.

"Hey, David!" Sozap shouted. "Yell something back so we know where you are!"

There was no reply.

"We better go look for him," Sozap said, trying to remain calm. It was hard to catch his breath. He reached into his pocket. "I've got a penlight."

Staying close together, the boys headed in the direction they had last heard David's voice. Every other jump, they called out his name. Only a glimmer of light showed now from behind the horizon. Without the help of Sozap's little flashlight, they would have been lost. Then, about twenty yards to their left, there was a large splashing sound, followed by a cry.

"Help! Somebody help me!" It was David.

Jumping from one cedar island to the next as quickly as they could, Billy and Sozap headed toward the sound of his cries.

"Help! Something has my leg!" David yelled.

Less than ten yards away now, the boys saw David. His arms were splashing the water around him. Although he was only a few feet from a small marshy island, he appeared unable to reach it. He was struggling to keep his head above the water.

"Hold on, David. We're almost there!" Sozap shouted.

Before they could reach him, David's cries were replaced by a gargling sound as his head slipped under the black water.

"He's gone under!" Billy yelled.

Both boys jumped into the water and swam toward the place where David had disappeared. Bubbles from his mouth rising to the surface, David's right hand broke the surface as he desperately reached toward land.

Both boys grabbed hold of David's arm.

"Pull," Sozap shouted, grabbing the roots of a cedar tree with one hand as he held David's sleeve with the other.

"He won't budge!" Billy said. "He must be stuck under a root!"

"Pull harder!"

Like a rock released from a sling, Billy and Sozap fell back onto the island. David, freed at last from under the water, landed directly on top of them.

"Get away from the water! Something . . . pulled me under!" David gasped.

Looking down into the dark water, for a split second Sozap thought he saw something move just under the surface. It looked almost like a brown, long-fingered hand. Then it was gone. Sozap shone his light into the water. There was nothing to be seen, but a chill went down his spine. He moved farther back onto the little island.

Once David had caught his breath, all three boys, soaked to the bone but guided by Sozap's flashlight, headed for the edge of the bog as quickly as they could. When they had reached the safety of the field, David told Billy and Sozap about the strange sound he had heard before falling in.

"It was something," he said, "a lot like singing."

It had gotten so loud he no longer heard their voices from the shore. Trying to find his own way back, he had slipped and fallen into the bog.

"And when I fell in the water," he said, "something grabbed my leg and pulled me under."

"You sure it wasn't a tree root or something?" Billy asked in a nervous voice.

"No, I swear something had hold of me. It let go after you guys grabbed my arm!" David looked over at Sozap, but Sozap said nothing about what he thought he'd seen.

It was just my imagination, Sozap said to himself. But as he thought about that brown long-fingered hand, a chill went down his back again.

Once out of the woods, the boys headed for their separate homes. Each one agreed they wouldn't tell anyone about what had happened to them. And, even though Billy and Sozap were never quite sure if David's story was true, none of them ever returned to the cedar bog.

TOAD WOMAN (ABENAKI)

Toad Woman is a monster described as a combination of a giant toad and an old woman who lives in the deep cedar swamps. She lures people in with her sweet voice. Because she has no teeth, she pulls her victims down into the mud and leaves them there until she can suck the rotten flesh off their bones. However, she is a coward and will only attack someone when they are alone and unaware. Stories of Toad Woman were often a very effective means of keeping children out of the dangerous swamps.

Sources:

Unpublished oral tradition: told by Abenaki elders Maurice Dennis and Stephen Laurent.

The Algonquin Legends of New England, by Charles G. Leland (Boston: Houghton and Mifflin, 1884).

APPENDIX

Abenaki *(Abenaki)* [Ab'-en-ah-key or Ah-ben'-ah-key] People of northern New England; literally "People of the Dawn Land"

Aglebemu *(Abenaki)* [Ag-luh-bem'-oo] Water monster

Aiyannoweh *(Oneida)* [Ay-yahn-no'-wey] "Swift Runner"

Akon:wara *(Mohawk)* [Ah-gohn-wah'-rah] "Ugly Face"

Amankamek *(Lenape)* [Ah-man'-kah-mehk] Giant horned snake

Awanootsak *(Abenaki)* [Ah-wah-noots'-ak] European Americans; literally, "Who are these people?"

Awasos *(Abenaki)* [Ah-wah'-sos] Bear

Azon *(Abenaki)* [Ah-zone'] John

Chenoo *(Passamaquoddy)* [Chay'-noo] Cannibal giant

Dagwaynonyent *(Seneca)* [Dah-gweh'-nohn-
yent] Flying head

Genonsgwa *(Seneca)* [Geh-nohns'-gwa] Stone
giant; literally "flint coat"

Gluskabe *(Penobscot)* [Gloos-kah'-bey] Changer hero; literally, "The Talker"

Kahnesatake *(Mohawk)* [Kah-nuh-suh-dah'-
gey] Mohawk village; literally, "By the
Rapids"

Kasko *(Abenaki)* [Kahs-ko'] A man's name

Keewahkwee *(Penobscot)* [Key-wah-kwee]
Cannibal ogre

Kitselemukong *(Lenape)* [Kiht'-see-luh-moo-
kong'] The Creator; literally, "Great Mystery"

Kwanitewk *(Abenaki)* [Kwah-nee-tewk']
The Connecticut River; literally, "Long
River"

Lenape *(Lenape)* [Leh-nah'-pay] People of the
lower Hudson Valley, New Jersey, Dela-

ware, Pennsylvania; literally, "Human Beings"

Mahican *(Mahican)* [Ma-hee'-cun] Northern relations of the Lenape; literally, "Where the Tide Flows Upriver"

Mamuui *(Lenape)* [Mah'-moo-oo-ee] The Eater; cannibal monster

Mohawk *(Algonquin)* [Mo'-hawk] Eastern-most Iroquois nation; "The Flint People"

Nolka *(Abenaki)* [Nol'-kah] Deer

Oneida *(Oneida)* [Oh-ni'-dah] Iroquois nation between the Mohawk and Onondaga; "Standing Stone People."

Onondaga *(Onondaga)* [On-on-dah'-gah] Central Iroquois nation; "People of the Hills"

Odanak *(Abenaki)* [Oh'-dah-nak] A northern Abenaki village near Quebec; literally, "Little Village"

Passamaquoddy *(Passamaquoddy)* (Pass-uh-mah-kwah'-dey] People of eastern Maine; literally, "Plenty of Pollack"

Penobscot *(Penobscot)* [Pen-ahb'-skaht] People of central and western Maine; literally, "Many Stones"

Pitolo *(Abenaki)* [Pih-to'-lo] Peter

Seneca *(Algonquin)* [Sen'-eh-ka] Westernmost Iroquois nation; "People of the Stone"

Skunny-Wundy *(Seneca)* [Skuh'-nee Wun'-dee] Seneca trickster hero; literally, "Cross-the-Creek"

Sozap *(Abenaki)* [So'-zap] Joseph

Wu *(Seneca)* [Woo] An exclamation equivalent to "Who's there?"

Yakwawiak *(Lenape)* [Yah-kwa'-wee-ahk] Giant mastodon